I LOVE TO EAT FRUITS AND VEGETABLES

난 과일과 야채를 정말 좋아해요

Shelley Admont

Illustrated by Sonal Goyal, Sumit Sakhuja

First edition, 2016
Translated from English by Christine Park
번역 박다솜

I Love to Eat Fruits and Vegetables (Korean Bilingual Edition)/ Shelley Admont
ISBN: 978-1-77268-323-3 paperback
ISBN: 978-1-77268-438-4 hardcover
ISBN: 978-1-77268-322-6 eBook

Please note that the Korean and English versions of the story have been written to be as
close as possible. However, in some cases they differ in order to accommodate nuances
and fluidity of each language.

Although the author and the publisher have made every effort to ensure the accuracy and
completeness of information contained in this book, we assume no responsibility for errors,
inaccuracies, omission, inconsistency, or consequences from such information.

for those I love the most
내가 가장 사랑하는 사람들에게

It was an hour before lunch. Jimmy, a little bunny, was playing with his two older brothers.

점심을 먹기 한 시간 전이었어요. 작은 토끼 지미는 두 형들과 놀고 있었죠.

"I really feel like eating something sweet," said Jimmy suddenly.

"나는 단 것이 먹고 싶어," 갑자기 지미가 말했어요.

"We can't eat candy before lunch," said the oldest brother. "You know we're not allowed, Jimmy."

"하지만 점심을 먹기 전에 사탕을 먹으면 안 돼." 지미의 큰 형이 말했어요. "엄마가 안 된다고 하실 거 너도 알잖아."

"I like apples and grapes," said the middle brother. "They're sweet and tasty."

"나는 사과랑 포도가 좋아." 지미의 둘째 형이 말했어요. "달고 맛있잖아."

Jimmy curled his lip. "Yuck, I don't like eating fruits."

지미가 입술을 삐쭉 내밀었어요. "우웩, 난 과일이 싫어."

Then he whispered, "Guess what? I saw that Mom bought some new candy yesterday. I'm going to take some. Who's joining me?"

그러고는 지미가 속삭였어요. "그거 알아? 엄마가 어제 사탕을 사 온 걸 내가 봤어. 나랑 같이 사탕 몇 개를 가져다 먹을 사람?"

"Not me," said his oldest brother and went back to his toys.

"난 안 할거야." 지미의 큰 형이 이렇게 말하고 다시 장난감을 가지고 놀기 시작했어요.

"I'm not coming either," replied his middle brother.

"나도 안 해." 둘째 형도 말했어요.

Jimmy waved his hand and left the room.
지미가 손을 흔들고 방을 나섰어요.

Slowly, he made his way to the kitchen, looking around to check that nobody was watching.
그러고는 누가 보지는 않을까 주변을 살피며 천천히 주방으로 걸어 갔어요.

The table was already prepared for lunch.
식탁에는 이미 점심이 차려져 있었어요.

Each bunny had his own plate. The oldest brother had the blue plate, and the middle brother had the green one. The orange plate was for Jimmy.

식탁 위에는 첫째 토끼를 위한 파란색 접시, 둘째 토끼를 위한 초록색 접시, 그리고 지미를 위한 주황색 접시가 있었어요.

In the center of the table was a big bowl filled with fresh vegetables. There were cucumbers, carrots, tomatoes, red and yellow peppers, and some cabbage.

식탁 한 가운데에는 싱싱한 야채가 있는 커다란 그릇이 놓여 있었어요. 그 안에는 오이, 당근, 토마토, 빨간색과 노란색 파프리카, 그리고 상추가 있었어요.

Jimmy scrunched his nose. Ugh! I'm not going to eat THAT, he thought.

지미가 코끝을 찡그리며 생각했어요. 으으! 난 저걸 절대로 먹지 않을 테야.

He went over to the cupboard and spotted the bag of candy. But the cupboard was so high that Jimmy was unable to reach it.

찬장으로 걸어간 지미가 사탕 봉지를 발견했어요.
하지만, 찬장이 너무 높아서 지미의 손이 닿지
않았어요.

He took one of the chairs and moved it nearer to the cupboard. He climbed up onto it, but he still wasn't able to reach the shelf!

의자 하나를 찬장으로 가까이 가져가 그 위에
올라섰지만, 그래도 손이 닿지 않았어요.

Jimmy got back down and looked around again. This time, he took a large empty pot and turned it upside down. He put the pot on the chair and then climbed up.

지미가 의자에서 내려와 주위를 둘러 보았어요.

이번에는 커다란 냄비를 뒤집어서 의자 위에 올리고 그 위에 올라 섰어요.

Now, he was able to see the highest shelf. In the far corner of the shelf, there it was a huge bag full of candy! But...he still wasn't able to touch it. He needed to be a tiny bit higher.

이렇게 하자 가장 높은 선반이 보이기 시작했어요.

선반 구석에 커다란 사탕 봉지가 보였어요! 하지만 이번에도 지미는 사탕 봉지를 잡을 수가 없었어요.

조금만 더 높이 올라 가면 될 텐데 말이에요.

What else can I use? thought Jimmy while getting down. Suddenly, he saw his mom's huge cookbook.

어떻게 해야 더 높이 올라갈 수 있을까? 지미가 내려오면서 생각했어요. 그 순간, 엄마의 커다란 요리책이 보였어요.

"That's exactly what I need!" he said happily as he grabbed the book.

"그래, 바로 저거야!" 지미가 기쁜 목소리로 소리를 지르며 요리책을 집어 들었어요.

He put the cookbook on the upside-down pot and slowly climbed up. Now he was able to touch the shelf.

지미가 커다란 요리책을 뒤집어진 냄비 위에 올리고 그 위에 올라갔어요. 이번에는 선반에 손이 닿았어요.

But as Jimmy reached for the bag of candy, the chair began to rock. Jimmy quickly lost his balance and fell flat on the ground.

하지만 지미가 사탕 봉지를 향해 손을 뻗는 순간, 의자가 흔들리기 시작했어요. 지미가 중심을 잃고 바닥에 떨어졌어요.

The pot fell next to him with a loud bang. The cookbook came next, and it landed right on poor Jimmy's head.

그 순간, 냄비가 펑 하는 소리와 함께 지미 옆에 떨어졌어요. 그 다음에는 요리책이 지미의 얼굴 옆에 떨어졌어요.

Jimmy looked up at the cupboard and it seemed as if it was getting higher and higher. When he tried to stand up on his feet, he felt dizzy and had to sit back down.

지미가 올려다 봤을 때 찬장이 점점 높아지는 것 같았어요. 발을 딛고 일어나려고 했지만 너무 어지러워서 그만 주저앉고 말았어요.

At that exact moment, his two older brothers came into the kitchen. "What was that noise," they asked, "and where's Jimmy?"

바로 그 순간, 지미의 형들이 부엌으로 들어왔어요. "방금 무슨 소리였지," 큰 형이 물었어요, "그리고 지미는 어디 있지?"

Jimmy waved his hand. "I'm here!"
지미가 손을 흔들며 말했어요. "나 여기 있어!"

"How did you get so tiny?" asked his middle brother.
"너 왜 그렇게 작아진 거야?" 작은 형이 물었어요.

Only then did Jimmy realize why everything looked so big. He had become as small as a mouse!
바로 그때 지미는 모든 것이 엄청나게 커졌다는 걸 알아챘어요. 지미가 쥐만큼 작아진 것이었어요!

"I just climbed up to get some candy," he cried, "and then I fell down."
"난 그냥 사탕을 가지러 올라갔을 뿐이야," 지미가 외쳤어요, "그리고 떨어졌어."

"Maybe that's what caused you to become so little!" exclaimed the middle brother.
"그래서 그렇게 작아진 건가 봐!" 작은 형이 소리쳤어요.

"Oh, no! Will I stay this small forever?" Jimmy began crying.

"안돼! 그럼 나 영원히 이대로 살아야 하는 거야?" 지미가 울음을 터뜨렸어요.

"Don't cry," said the oldest brother. "We will figure something out. Let's just clean up before Mom comes in."

"울지 마," 큰 형이 말했어요. "방법을 찾아보자. 일단 엄마가 오기 전에 다 치우자."

Just as they finished putting everything back in its place, their mother walked into the kitchen.

모든 것을 제자리에 갖다 놓기 시작한 그때, 엄마가 부엌으로 걸어 들어오셨어요.

"We're going to eat lunch soon. Where's Jimmy?" Jimmy hid behind his older brothers.

"조금 있다가 점심을 먹을 거야. 지미는 어디 있니?" 지미는 형들 뒤로 숨어 버렸어요.

"Uh, uh..." stuttered his middle brother while thinking of something to say.

"어, 어…" 작은 형이 더듬거리며 뭐라고 말할까 생각했어요.

But the older brother was very smart. "Mom, if someone wants to grow quickly and be tall and strong, what would he need to do?" he asked.

그때 똑똑한 큰 형이 말했어요. "엄마, 키가 빨리 크고 힘이 세지고 싶을 땐 어떻게 해야 해요?"

"He needs to eat his fruits and vegetables," she answered. "They contain lots of vitamins and minerals that help the body grow faster."

"과일과 야채를 많이 먹어야지," 엄마가 말했어요. "과일과 야채에는 비타민과 영양분이 많이 들어 있어서 빨리 자라게 해 주지."

"Now, you can sit down at the table and I will call Dad and Jimmy," their mother said and walked out of the kitchen.

"자, 이제 어서 앉아. 엄마가 가서 아빠랑 지미를 불러올게," 엄마가 부엌을 나서며 말했어요.

The oldest brother turned around to Jimmy. "Quick! You have to eat your fruits and vegetables."

큰 형이 지미를 향해 돌아섰어요. "어서! 과일과 야채를 먹어야해!"

"No way!" screamed Jimmy, "I don't even like fruits or vegetables!"

"싫어!" 지미가 소리쳤어요. "과일과 야채는 정말 싫어!"

"Do you want to stay this way forever then?" his middle brother asked.

"너 계속 그렇게 있고 싶어?" 작은 형이 물었어요.

"Of course not!" replied Jimmy.

"당연히 아니지!" 지미가 말했어요.

"So eat some vegetables," said the oldest brother. "Maybe you'll even like them."
He took a carrot from the plate on the table and slipped it in Jimmy's mouth.

"그럼 어서 야채를 먹어," 큰 형이 말했어요. "먹어 보면 좋아할 수도 있잖아." 큰 형이 당근 하나를 집어서 지미의 입에 넣어 주었어요.

"Ummm...this is sweet and tasty," Jimmy said as he chewed his carrot with his strong, white teeth.
"음…이거 달고 맛있는걸," 지미가 튼튼하고 흰 이로 당근을 씹어 먹으며 말했어요.

All of the sudden, he felt a strange tingly feeling spreading all over his body—it was just like magic.
그 순간 갑자기, 온몸이 따끔거리기 시작했어요 - 마법처럼 말이에요.

"Jimmy, look! You've grown a bit!" shouted the oldest brother.
"그것 봐! 너 조금 자랐어!" 큰 형이 큰 소리로 말했어요.

The middle brother gave Jimmy a juicy cucumber from the bowl. "Here, eat something else," he said.
이번에는 작은 형이 오이 하나를 집어 지미에게 건네 주었어요. "이것도 한 번 먹어봐."

With every bite, he felt his body getting stronger and stronger. He was growing!

오이를 한 입 먹을 때마다 온몸이 튼튼해지고 힘이 세지는 게 느껴졌어요. 지미가 자라나고 있었어요!

"You're finally yourself again," the oldest brother shouted and ran over to hug Jimmy.

"이제 돌아왔네," 큰 형이 기쁜 마음으로 소리를 지며 달려와 지미를 안아 주었어요.

His middle brother hugged him, too. "How are you feeling now?" he asked.

작은 형도 달려와 지미를 안아주며 물었어요. "기분이 어때?"

"I feel great and full of energy," Jimmy answered. "And you know what? These fruits and vegetables are really tasty. I should have tried them before!"

"힘이 솟아나는 기분이야," 지미가 대답했어요. "그리고 그거 알아? 과일과 야채들은 정말 맛있는 것 같아. 진작 먹을 걸 그랬어!"

All three brothers began to laugh loudly and jump around.

세 형제는 기분 좋게 웃으며 뛰어 다녔어요.

A few minutes later, Jimmy's parents entered the kitchen.
몇 분 후에, 지미의 부모님이 부엌으로 걸어 들어오셨어요.

"Great, everyone's here," said Dad.
"여기 있었구나," 아빠가 말했어요.

"I'm happy that everyone's in such a good mood," said Mom. "Don't forget to wash your hands!"
"모두가 기분이 좋은 것 같아 보기 좋구나," 엄마가 말했어요. "손 씻는 것을 잊지 말거라!"

The happy family sat around the large table and began eating all the tasty things there. Even Jimmy finished his whole plateful.
이렇게 행복한 다섯 가족은 큰 식탁에 들러 앉아 맛있는 음식을 먹기 시작했어요. 지미도 한 접시를 뚝딱 먹어 치웠죠.

From that day on, Jimmy liked eating all his fruits and vegetables. Sometimes, he still eats candy but only a little and only after his meals.

그 날 이후로 지미는 모든 과일과 야채를 맛있게 먹었어요. 가끔씩 사탕도 먹었지만 밥을 다 먹은 후에 아주 조금만 먹었답니다.